Library of Congress Cataloging in Publication Data
Bröger, Achim. Good morning, whale.
Translation of Guten Tag, lieber Wal.
[1. Whales—Fiction.   2. Friendship—Fiction]
I. Kalow, Gisela, illus.   II. Title.
PZ7.B78618Go   [E]   74-9762
ISBN 0-02-714460-7

GOOD MORNING, WHALE

BY ACHIM BRÖGER
PICTURES BY GISELA KALOW
TRANSLATED BY ELIZABETH SHUB

MACMILLAN PUBLISHING CO., INC.
NEW YORK
Copyright ©1974 K. Thienemanns Verlag, Stuttgart

Karl and his wife sat on a bench in front of their house and looked out over the river. In the days when he was still a fisherman, he was on the water from dawn till dark and never had any time for himself. But now he had all the time he wanted, and he loved to sit by the river and daydream. Best of all he liked to imagine the sea. It began far away where the river ended.

One day, as they sat together, he said to his wife, "I would so like to have a look at the sea."

"Why not go then?" she replied. "But don't stay too long. It's so nice to sit here with you on our bench."

They decided Karl should leave at once and began to get his boat ready for the journey.

When they had finished, Karl said goodbye to his wife and climbed into his boat.

"If you see a whale," she said, "say hello for me."

She stood on the dock and waved for a long time. Karl watched her as she grew smaller and smaller. Now she was so small that she could fit under Karl's cap. Soon she was as tiny as a drop of water, and finally Karl could no longer see her at all. Karl rowed on and on, and after a time he could smell the sea.

Karl knew he had reached the sea when he rowed his boat through waves much higher than any he had ever seen in the river. The sun shone and there were fish everywhere. He rowed on, but now and then he stopped to rest and watch the fish.

A large ship appeared on the horizon. It came closer and closer.
Karl's small boat was rocked by the waves it made. For a moment
Karl was afraid the boat would capsize. Then the ship sailed away.
Karl was alone again with the water, the fish and the sun.

He travelled on. When evening came,
the moon rose over the water and shone on
the boat. Karl had eaten his supper and was
getting sleepy. It was quiet on the sea.
Waves splashed around the boat, their crests
sparkling in the moonlight. The boat rocked
softly. Karl slept and dreamed all night long.

When he awoke, he saw an island before him.
But the island bobbed up and it had an eye.
It rose higher and it had a mouth. It seemed
a most unusual island. Karl blinked and
strained to have a good look. He was
astonished to discover that the island was
a whale.
"Good morning," Karl said, lifting his cap.
"My wife said to say hello. My name is Karl."

The huge creature gave Karl a whale of a
smile and thanked him for his wife's greeting.
Then he introduced himself.
"Whale," he said, wagging his tail politely.
They exchanged stories and jokes and en-
tertained one another.
Karl told the whale about his wife, about the
river, about birds and sunflowers. The whale
told Karl about flying fish, sharks and giant
turtles.
They stayed together for a night and a day.
The hours passed quickly, and it was time
for Karl to start for home.

The friends gave one another their addresses.
"Nine, Dock Street, Springdale. It's right on
the river," Karl said.
The whale said, "The Sea."
Karl headed his boat towards the river and
home to his wife.
From then on, he visited his friend the whale
every six months to the day. He was very
punctual.

But once when it was time for Karl's visit, he didn't come. The whale waited. He searched the waves. Karl and his boat did not appear. I must go and find out what has happened, the worried whale decided. He started out, but he was so nervous he lost his way, and instead of swimming into the river he found himself in a crowded harbour.

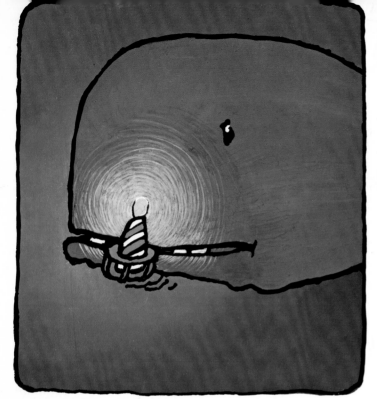 

He swam out of the harbour and made his way along the coast.
He came to a buoy. "Good day," he said. "Can you tell me
where the river begins?" The buoy did not answer. Only the
chain that held it clanked a bit. After a time he came to a lighthouse. "Good day," he said. "Can you direct me to the mouth
of the river?" The lighthouse too did not answer. It just stood
there, flashing its lights. But as it happened, the river began
just there, and the whale swam right into it. As he travelled
along, he noticed that the river was getting narrower and
narrower.

Suddenly, just as he was passing by a town, he got stuck beneath a bridge. The people gathered around. "A big whale in our small town," they said, astonished. "Who could have imagined such a thing?"

They tried to tow the whale from under the bridge. They tried to push him out. But nothing helped. They stroked him to comfort him.

For days the whale lay under the bridge and thought of Karl.
He was so upset he ate nothing. "See how sad his eyes look,"
the people said. They noticed that the whale was getting
thinner and thinner.

In a few days he had lost so much weight he was able to swim
out from under the bridge. The people came out of their
houses and gathered at the river. The town band played and
the whale wagged his tail and swam on.

But the river continued to grow narrower and narrower. The
whale would not eat and he grew smaller and smaller. It can't
be long before I reach Springdale, he thought to himself.

And soon the whale caught sight of Karl sitting on his bench, and almost at the same time Karl saw him. Karl had a plaster cast on his leg.

"How wonderful that you have come to visit me," he called. "I was getting the boat ready to go to see you when I tripped over an oar. I broke my leg. But what has made you shrink so? You must tell me all about it, just as soon as I fetch a jar to put you in."

Karl limped to his house and got a large jar. He hurried
back and dipped the jar in the river so that the whale
could swim into it. When the whale was safely inside,
Karl carefully carried the jar to his wife.

"We have a visitor, swimming right here in this jar," he
said. "It's my friend the whale."

Karl's wife clasped her head in both hands. "My good-
ness!" she exclaimed. "Actually I had imagined your
friend the whale as somewhat bigger. But how very nice
that he is here!"

They went into the living room and settled down to talk.
They agreed that when the whale started eating and
began to grow again, Karl would take him back to the sea.
By then, too, Karl's leg would be mended. But for the
moment neither the whale nor Karl wanted to think about
it. They had so much to tell one another.